Denise & Kendra Talley

"YOU CAN DO IT TOO!!!"

USTRATED BY TREVIUS BRINSON

 FriesenPress

Suite 300 - 990 Fort St
Victoria, BC, V8V 3K2
Canada

www.friesenpress.com

Copyright © 2021 by Denise and Kendra Talley
First Edition — 2021

All rights reserved.

Cover and Book Illustrations by Trevius Brinson

Edited by Keya Talley

This is a work of creative nonfiction. Some parts have been fictionalized in varying degrees, for varying purposes.

Photography by J. Ever Productions (foz1993@gmail.com)

No part of this publication may be reproduced in any form, or by any means, electronic or mechanical, including photocopying, recording, or any information browsing, storage, or retrieval system, without permission in writing from FriesenPress.

ISBN
978-1-5255-9314-7 (Hardcover)
978-1-5255-9313-0 (Paperback)
978-1-5255-9315-4 (eBook)

1. JUVENILE NONFICTION, BIOGRAPHY & AUTOBIOGRAPHY

Distributed to the trade by The Ingram Book Company

This book was inspired by Kameron Ramir Talley.

We dedicate this book to our heavenly Father, Jesus Christ,
who has blessed our family with incredible people.
We also dedicate this to our ancestors who have paved the way and
allowed us to think outside the box, encouraging us to explore our horizons.
We must all do our part to make a difference in this world.

Hi, my name is Ramir.
I am nine years old, and I attend Hollingsworth Elementary School.
I am African-American, and my family taught me to be proud of who I am.

Living with my mom and three sisters can be eventful. I am comical and like to entertain my family by making them laugh with my jokes. I'm the young man of the house.

My family teaches me very useful lessons. I love my family very much.

I love to read comic books, watch movies, play sports, and spend time with my family.

Even though it may seem like I have a cool life,
being me can be tough sometime.
When I was little, I was diagnosed with a learning disability.
Later, we found out that I was autistic.

Having autism can make life hard sometimes.
I can be sensitive to loud noises and cover my hands over my ears when I hear them.

Like you, I must learn at my own pace, because I have unique needs.

For example, I like a lot of repetition.

Although autism is a part of me, I enjoy my life to the fullest.
I am caring, friendly, playful, and kind hearted.
At a young age, I embraced God's purpose for my life by keeping a positive attitude.
That is my superpower through which I am able to show love, kindness, and respect to others.
I am a special person!

My family taught me that staying active is an important part of life, especially if I want to keep growing into a healthy person!
The reason I wanted to join various sports is because it helped me make friends and become passionate about sports, and it improved my teamwork skills.
I participated in Cub Scouts, football and basketball.
I even worked my way up to a green belt in karate and taught myself to swim!
Although these are loud sports, by having a positive attitude I was able to push through the challenges.

Learning karate was a great help in boosting my confidence.
It taught me how to talk with bullies in school when I felt they were treating me unkindly.
I am a friendly person, but I don't like to get picked on or teased.

My mom makes sure I go to school every day. Sometimes that is hard for me, but thanks to my God-given superpower, I use my positive attitude to help me focus on doing my best. With practice, this led me to winning the perfect attendance award! I also made the honor roll and won "Most Improved."

I love God, and I know God loves me!
I enjoy going to church with my family.
My sister, cousins, and I all serve in the church.
We participate in plays and skits, and we sing in the youth choir.
With lots of hard work and determination, I know I can overcome obstacles in life,
because I know that I am fearfully and wonderfully made.
I was created by a God that loves me tremendously!
God made me to be awesome, just like him, and I must share my light with the world!

CPSIA information can be obtained at www.ICGtesting.com
Printed in the USA
BVIW121529190321
602996BV00008B/29